MONSTERS UNIVERSITY

DARE TO SCARE

ISBN 978-0-7364-3038-8 (trade)
ISBN 978-0-7364-8123-6 (lib. bdg.)

Printed in the United States of America
10 9 8 7 6 5 4 3 2 1

DISNEY · PIXAR

MONSTERS
UNIVERSITY

DARE TO SCARE

Adapted by Calliope Glass

Illustrated by David Gilson

Golden® First Chapters
g A GOLDEN BOOK • NEW YORK

CHAPTER 1

My name is Mike Wazowski. When I was six years old, my class took a field trip to Monsters, Incorporated. Before that trip, I was just Mike. But when I went to bed that night, I was Mike Wazowski: Future Scarer.

Back then, I was the smallest monster in my class, and my classmates didn't pay me much attention. Sometimes that got me down, but not that day. I was too excited.

"Now, stay close together," the tour guide said to our class as he led us into a giant room. "We're entering a very dangerous area. Welcome to the scare floor."

Monsters hurried around. They were bringing in scream canisters, setting up door stations, and checking checklists.

"Here is where we collect the scream energy to power our whole world," the tour guide said. Highly trained monsters called Scarers used special doors to sneak into human children's bedrooms and scare them.

The children's screams were collected and stored. Scaring was dangerous work because human children were toxic to monsters.

My heart skipped a beat when the Scarers walked onto the scare floor. They were so cool.

One of them stopped to talk to us. My teacher, Mrs. Graves, told him that we were there to learn what it took to be a Scarer.

The Scarer pointed to his baseball cap. It had the letters "MU" on it. "I learned everything I know from my school," he said. "Monsters

University. It's the best scaring school there is."

The Scarer walked toward the door stations. We were about to watch a real scare! But I was stuck behind the rest of my class.

"Come on, you guys! I want to see!" I said.

"Out of the way, Wazowski," said one of my classmates, pushing me aside. "You don't belong on a scare floor."

I do so! I thought. So I snuck over the safety line to get a better look.

As the Scarer with the MU cap approached a door, I inched closer to watch. He walked through the door, and before I realized what I was doing, I walked through with him!

The Scarer hadn't noticed me sneak in behind him. He crept around the edges of the room. He lurked. He loomed. And then he *ROARED!* It was the most awesome thing I had ever seen.

As the kid's scream was collected in a scream can, the Scarer moved quickly back through the door to Monsters, Inc. I followed him. My head was spinning.

At Monsters, Inc., a whole crowd was waiting for me—factory workers, security guards, and, of course, Mrs. Graves. They all began to yell when they saw me.

The Scarer I'd followed looked mad. "That was real dangerous, kid," he said sternly. "I

didn't even know you were in there." Then, to my surprise, he winked and gave me his Monsters University hat. Right then, I didn't care how much trouble I was in.

"Michael," Mrs. Graves said angrily, "what do you have to say for yourself?"

I smiled. "How do I become a Scarer?"

From that day on, my mind was made up. The best way to become a Scarer was to get into a great college, and I knew exactly where I wanted to go: Monsters University. I wore the Scarer's MU baseball cap all the time.

After years of hard work, all my studies paid off. I got in to Monsters University!

CHAPTER 2

It was my first day at Monsters University. As I walked onto campus, I looked around at all the grand buildings. I saw giant monsters riding bikes and playing Frisbee, aquatic monsters swimming through the school's canals, and winged monsters sailing through the air.

After registration, I went to the activities fair. As I was walking by the Greek Council booth, the monster behind the table said, "We sponsor the annual Scare Games."

"The what?" I went closer to find out more.

The Greek Council president and vice president were the heads of all the fraternities and sororities, the special social clubs at MU. They told me more about the games. "They're a super-intense scaring competition. You get a chance to prove you're the best!" the VP said.

Well, I *did* plan to be the best. So I grabbed a flyer and headed to the dorms.

As I approached my room, my heart started to beat a little faster. I was about to meet my new roommate. *My new lifelong best friend could be in there,* I thought.

When I opened the door, I saw a monster standing in the shadows. He was tall, with purple scales and glasses.

"Hi, I'm Randy Boggs, scaring major," he said, holding out a friendly hand.

I thought Randy seemed nice, but he was pretty nervous. Every time something startled him, he'd disappear by blending into the background.

As we settled into the room, I went through my

checklist. "Unpack: check," I said. "Hang posters: check. Now I just need to ace my classes, graduate with honors, and become the greatest Scarer ever."

"I wish I had your confidence, Mike," Randy said. "Aren't you even a little nervous?"

"Actually, no," I said, looking out the window at the splendid campus. "I've been waiting for this my whole life."

The next morning, I hurried to my first class: Scaring 101. It was held in the School of Scaring, the grandest building on campus.

Climbing the steps, I was in awe. Some of the

greatest Scarers in history had passed through those doors. In the lecture hall, I spotted a statue of Professor Hardscrabble, the dean of the School of Scaring. She was a living legend. A scream canister containing her record-breaking scream sat right below her statue.

I took a seat in the front row. Just as Professor Knight was introducing himself to the class, a shadow fell over the room. A huge, winged monster landed in front of us. It was Dean Hardscrabble!

"I just thought I'd drop by to see the terrifying faces joining us this year," she said. Her many legs tapped against the stone floor as she paced in front of us. "Scariness is the true measure of a monster. If you're not scary, what kind of monster are you?"

There was a long, nervous silence as the class waited for her to go on.

"At the end of the semester," Dean Hardscrabble said, "there will be a final exam. Fail that exam, and you are out of the Scaring Program."

With that chilling statement, Dean Hardscrabble left, flying through an opening in the domed ceiling of the lecture hall.

As the students murmured, Professor Knight stepped forward and clapped his hands. "All right, who can tell me the principles of an effective roar?" he asked.

I raised my hand tentatively.

The professor called on me. I had just launched into the answer when—

"ROAAAAAAAAAR!"

It was the fiercest roar I'd ever heard. Everyone in the room turned to see who it had come from.

CHAPTER 3

A huge monster stood in the doorway. He had blue fur with purple spots, long horns, and big claws.

"Whoops, sorry," he said with a laugh. "I heard someone say 'roar,' so I just kinda went for it." He squeezed between students, looking for an empty seat.

Professor Knight appeared surprised. "Very impressive, Mr. . . ."

"Sullivan. Jimmy Sullivan. You can call me Sulley," the blue monster replied. The guy had confidence oozing from his ears. It turned out he was the son of Bill Sullivan, a scaring legend.

All eyes in the classroom were on that big blue lug. Even the professor had forgotten about me. "I'm sorry," I said to Professor Knight, "should I keep going?"

"No," he replied. "Mr. Sullivan covered it."

Sulley just smirked. He slumped down into a seat, then turned to the student next to him. "Could I borrow a pencil?" he whispered. "I forgot all my stuff."

The student gave Sulley a pencil, and he began to pick his teeth with it.

I didn't think Sulley and I were going to be friends.

By that night, though, I'd forgotten all about Sulley. After a full day of classes, my head was whirling. Randy wanted me to go to a party with him, but I decided to study instead. The scaring final was only months away, and I wasn't taking any chances.

I had just opened my books when suddenly a weird creature popped through my open window. It ran around the room, knocking things over. Then it darted under the bed.

A second later, *another* face appeared in my window. Sulley! He climbed in and ducked beneath the windowsill.

"Hey!" I said. "What are you—"

Sulley shushed me. I looked outside and saw a bunch of guys wearing jackets from Fear Tech, MU's rival school.

"That guy's in big trouble," one growled. I realized they were looking for Sulley.

"Hey, guys, over here!" another Fear Tech student yelled. They ran off.

Sulley laughed. "Fear Tech dummies."

"Why are you in my room?" I demanded.

"*Your* room? This is my—" Sulley looked around. "This is not my room."

A squeal came from under the bed. "Archie, come here, boy," Sulley said.

"Archie?" I asked.

"Archie the Scare Pig. Fear Tech's mascot," Sulley explained. "I stole it! I'm going to take it to Roar Omega Roar—the top fraternity on campus." He lifted the bed. Archie shot out and jumped up on the bookcase, which came crashing down on top of me and Sulley.

Sulley just laughed. "I haven't introduced myself," he said. "James P. Sullivan."

"Mike Wazowski," I replied coldly. "Listen, it was quite delightful meeting you, but if you don't mind, I have to study my scaring."

"Pssh," Sulley scoffed. "You don't need to study scaring, you just *do* it."

The guy was really starting to get on my nerves. I was about to tell him to buzz off when Archie snatched my MU cap and dove out the window.

"My hat!" I yelled, jumping after him.

"My pig!" Sulley yelled, following.

That pig was fast! I leaped onto his back, but it didn't even slow him down. Instead, I found myself *riding* Archie. He ran all the way to Frat Row, the block where all the fraternity houses stood. We barreled through Roar Omega Roar's party.

Finally, I fell off Archie. Thinking fast, I grabbed a football and threw it at a row of bikes.

The bikes toppled like dominoes. They knocked over a trash can. Archie skidded right into it!

"Got it!" I cried as I grabbed my hat.

"MU rules!" Sulley lifted Archie and me into the air. Around us, students cheered.

A huge monster wearing a ROR jacket walked over. "Johnny Worthington, president of Roar Omega Roar," he said. "Any freshman with the guts to pull off a stunt like that has got 'Future Scarer' written all over him."

Johnny put his arm around Sulley and led him toward the ROR fraternity house. I started to walk with them. After all, I was the one who'd caught Archie.

"Sorry, killer," Johnny said, leaning down to look at me, "but you might want to hang out with someone a little more your speed. Those guys look like fun."

Johnny pointed to a few fraternity brothers

standing by a table with balloons and cake. They were the least scary-looking bunch I'd ever seen.

"Oh, hey there!" one of them called. "Want to join Oozma Kappa?"

I couldn't believe Johnny was lumping me in with those guys. "Is that a joke?" I asked.

"This is a party for *scare students,*" Sulley told me.

"I *am* a scare student!" I was getting really mad.

"I mean for scare students who actually stand a chance," Sulley said.

That was it. I had *had* it with this guy. "My chances are as good as yours," I said. "I'm going to scare circles around you this year."

Sulley just laughed. "I'd like to see that."

"Oh, don't worry," I said. I put on my trusty old MU hat and walked away. "You will."

CHAPTER 4

For the rest of the semester, I studied harder than I'd ever studied before. I practically *lived* in the library. It began to pay off. I got As on my quizzes. And I noticed that Sulley was getting Cs. We'd see who the real Scarer was.

When the day of the final exam arrived, I was ready.

"Today's final will judge your ability to perform the appropriate scare . . . in the scare simulator." Professor Knight gestured to the center of the lecture hall, where a simulator had been set up. The simulator was a training room for testing how scary a monster could be. It was decorated like a human child's bedroom. There was even a robotic dummy that screamed. The scarier you were, the higher a score you got in the simulator.

One by one, students were called to the center of the room to perform their scares. I saw Dean Hardscrabble enter the lecture hall. She silently watched the exams.

While I waited for my turn, I practiced in a corner. Suddenly, Sulley brushed past me, knocking my books to the floor.

"Hey, do you mind?" I snapped.

"Don't mind at all," Sulley said with a smirk.

"Stay out of my way. Unlike you, I had to work hard to get into the Scaring Program," I told him.

"That's because you don't belong here," Sulley shot back.

I roared in Sulley's face, just to show him.

He flinched, then roared back. Before I knew it, we were having a roaring contest during the final exam, right in front of Dean Hardscrabble.

Suddenly, Sulley tripped over one of my books on the floor and bumped into the statue of Dean Hardscrabble. The scream canister—the one that contained her record-setting scream—began to wobble. We watched in horror as it fell and hit the floor. It exploded, shooting into the air and releasing the scream inside.

The can banged all over the room. Students ducked as it whizzed past their heads.

When the scream finally faded, a terrible silence hung over the lecture hall. Dean Hardscrabble swooped down to us.

"I'm so sorry," I said.

"It was an accident," Sulley added.

Professor Hardscrabble picked up the broken scream can. She seemed surprisingly calm.

"Accidents happen. The important thing is no one got hurt," she said.

"You're taking this remarkably well," I said nervously.

"Let's continue the exams," Hardscrabble said. "Mr. Wazowski, I'm a five-year-old girl on a farm in Kansas afraid of lightning. Which scare do you use?"

I was confused. What about the simulator?

"Which scare do you use?" she repeated.

"A Shadow Approach with a Crackle Holler."

"Demonstrate."

I took a deep breath—

"Stop!" Hardscrabble ordered. "I've seen enough." She turned to Sulley. "I'm a seven-year-old boy—" But Sulley interrupted her with a roar.

Hardscrabble didn't flinch. "I wasn't finished," she said.

"I don't need to know any of that stuff to scare," Sulley boasted.

"That 'stuff' would have informed you that this particular child is afraid of snakes," Hardscrabble told him. "So a roar wouldn't make him scream. It would make him cry, alerting his parents, exposing the monster world, and destroying life as we know it. So I'm afraid I cannot recommend that you continue in the Scaring Program."

"But I'm a Sullivan!" cried Sulley.

"Then I'm sure your family will be very disappointed," she said.

Hardscrabble turned back to me. "And you, Mr. Wazowski, what you lack is something that cannot be taught. You're not scary. You will not be continuing in the Scaring Program."

CHAPTER 5

The next few weeks were the worst of my life. Everything I'd worked for was gone. And it was all Sulley's fault.

I was almost ready to give up on college for good. Then I happened to see the Scare Games flyer, the one I'd picked up on the first day of school. Suddenly, I had an idea. This was my chance to prove myself. The Scare Games could turn everything around for me.

There was no time to lose. Sign-ups were happening that day!

I went to Frat Row and saw a huge crowd. All the fraternities and sororities were there.

Dean Hardscrabble was there, too, giving a speech to kick off the games.

"As a student, I created these games as a friendly competition," she declared. "But be prepared: to take home the trophy, you must be the most fearsome monsters on campus."

"All right, everybody," the Greek Council VP announced, "sign-ups for the Scare Games are officially—"

"I'm signing up!" I yelled. Behind me, I heard Johnny Worthington and the ROR brothers burst out laughing. I ignored them.

"You have to be in a fraternity to compete," the VP said.

I'd already thought of that. "Behold," I said, "the next winning fraternity of the Scare Games: the brothers, my brothers, of Oozma Kappa!"

"Mr. Wazowski." Hardscrabble's voice rang out over the crowd. "What are you doing?"

"How about a little wager?" I asked her. "If I win, you let me back in the Scaring Program."

I heard surprised gasps from the crowd. But Hardscrabble played it cool. "Very well, if you win, I will let your entire team into the Scaring Program. But if you lose, you will pack up your things and leave Monsters University."

"Deal," I said.

"Now," said Hardscrabble, "all you need to do is find enough members to compete."

To compete in the games, each team needed six monsters. With me, Oozma Kappa only had five. We were still one monster short.

I spotted Randy and begged him to join our team. I was amazed to hear he'd already joined a fraternity—the RORs.

"Your team doesn't qualify," the Greek Council president said.

"Yes, it does," a deep voice suddenly

declared. "The star player has just arrived."

I turned to see Sulley. After he'd blown the final, the RORs didn't want him anymore.

"No way! Anyone else!" I exclaimed. But there was no one else. I needed him on my team.

"Good luck," Hardscrabble said in a way that made me shiver.

Ⓜ

As soon as I entered the Oozma Kappa fraternity house, I wondered if I had made a mistake. Right away, I could tell something was wrong. There were knickknacks and doilies everywhere. It looked like my grandmother's house!

"As the president of Oozma Kappa, it is my honor to welcome you to your new home," said a monster named Don, who was almost as old as my dad.

Terri and Terry introduced themselves next. They were brothers with one body and two heads. I guess they were tired of always being together. They bickered most of the time.

"Hey, I'm Art!" said a furry purple monster, stepping forward. "I'm excited to live with you, and laugh with you, and cry with you." Art was a New Age philosophy major. Not exactly Scarer material.

"Guess that leaves me," said a little guy, popping up behind Sulley and startling him. "My friends call me Squishy. I'm undeclared,

unattached, and . . . unwelcome pretty much everywhere but here." The OK fraternity house was Squishy's mom's house. That explained the doilies.

Since we were the newest members, Sulley and I had to share a room. As soon as we were alone, Sulley turned to me and hissed, "Are you kidding me?"

"Look," I said, "they don't have to be good. I'm going to carry the whole team."

"Really?" Sulley said sarcastically. "And who's going to carry you?"

Sulley was only going to make this harder. I could already tell. But I'd learned my lesson at the Scaring 101 final. I couldn't let Sulley ruin my plans.

Anyway, we were about to find out if we had what it took. The next day, an invitation arrived for the first event in the Scare Games.

CHAPTER 6

The next night we made our way to a sewer tunnel below MU, where the first Scare Games event was taking place. The other teams were already there. Roar Omega Roar (ROR), Eta Hiss Hiss (HSS), Jaws Theta Chi (JOX), Python Nu Kappa (PNK), and Slugma Slugma Kappa (EEK).

"Welcome to your worst nightmare, the Scare Games," said the Greek Council vice president. "Let's begin the first competition: the Toxicity Challenge."

"Human kids are toxic!" said the president. "Anything they touch is toxic."

"We don't have any toxic toys, but thanks to

MU's biology department, we've found a close second," the VP added. "The stinging glow urchin!"

He used a pair of tongs to hold up a bright purple creature. Electric sparks gathered around the urchin's sharp spikes.

The president explained the rules. The teams had to race through a sewer tunnel filled with glow urchins. The team that came in last would be eliminated from the Games.

Squishy popped up behind me, startling me. "Does that mean if we lose we're out?"

"We're not going to lose. I'm going to win the race for us," I told him.

Sulley pushed me out of the way. "That's very cute," he said. "But *I'm* going to win this."

I headed for the starting line. This was my chance to finish what I'd begun and show Sulley who the better Scarer was.

"Attention!" said the president. "One last thing. Scarers work in the dark." The lights went out. The only light came from the crackling electric glow urchins.

"I wanna go home!" Squishy peeped.

"Ready!" the VP called.

I glared at Sulley.

"Set!"

He glared back.

"Go!"

I took off, weaving around the glowing urchins on the ground. I ducked as urchins came whizzing through the air, thrown by monsters above us. All the while I kept my eye on Sulley. For a big guy, he moved surprisingly fast.

"Ahh!" Sulley yelled as a flying urchin stung him on the shoulder. I jumped into the lead. I turned back to laugh at Sulley and—*yow!*—I stepped on an urchin and went down.

But I quickly got back up, limping on my swollen leg. I couldn't let Sulley beat me!

I managed a final burst of energy just as Sulley did. We sprinted across the finish line.

"Take that, Wazowski!" Sulley wheezed.

"Are you delirious? I beat you!" I shot back.

Then I noticed something. Everyone was laughing and pointing at us. I didn't get it. Sure, the RORs had finished first. But second place was nothing to laugh at, was it?

"Second place, Jaws Theta Chi!" the VP announced.

What?

"Your whole team has to cross the finish line," Johnny shouted.

Oh no. I couldn't do anything but watch as, one by one, the EEK, PNK, and HSS teams crossed the finish line. Finally, the rest of the Oozma Kappas straggled out of the tunnel. "Last place, Oozma Kappa!" the VP said.

"No!" I gasped. My last shot at becoming a Scarer was gone!

"Attention," the VP piped up suddenly. "Jaws Theta Chi has been disqualified!"

I looked up just in time to see a referee wipe protective gel off a JOX brother. JOX had cheated! They were out, and that meant—

"It's a miracle. Oozma Kappa is back in the game!" the VP declared.

I breathed a huge sigh of relief. Then I saw Hardscrabble glaring at me. "Your luck will run out eventually," she said.

I checked out my team. Bruised and swollen from their run-ins with the glow urchins, they looked less scary than ever.

Winning the Scare Games was going to be harder than I thought.

CHAPTER 7

After the first event, I knew I couldn't win the Scare Games on my own.

The second challenge, Avoid the Adult, was all about avoiding capture. In the world of real scaring, no Scarer wants to get caught by a kid's parent. So for this event, each team had to sneak through the Monsters University library and capture their flag while avoiding the librarian.

Earlier that day, I'd coached the team. "From now on, we are of one mind—my mind," I told them. "I will tell you exactly what to do and how to do it." I couldn't risk any of them messing up again.

That night, as the event got under way, we crept single file across the library's creaky floor and made our way toward the flags. They were hanging from the arm of a statue high up on the second-floor balcony.

We could see the librarian sitting at her desk. She looked like a harmless old monster.

Just then, a floorboard creaked as a student who was studying got up from his seat. The librarian whipped around. Then she rose up—and up and up. She was as tall as the building!

"Quiet!" the librarian growled, holding a finger to her lips. She snatched the poor student in her tentacles and tossed him out of the library through a hole in the domed roof.

It was one of the most frightening things I'd ever seen.

The team started to move faster. I could tell they wanted to get out of there.

But we couldn't risk blowing the race. "Do exactly what I do," I whispered. "Slow and steady."

"Slow and steady," they echoed, one after the other.

Around us, the other teams had already grabbed their flags. Sulley was getting impatient. Finally, he ran ahead.

"Sullivan!" I hissed.

"Sullivan!" the rest of the OKs echoed. I shushed them, but they only copied me. They were doing exactly what I did.

Meanwhile, Sulley had grabbed a bookshelf ladder and climbed up to the balcony. The ladder put him close to our flag, but he couldn't quite reach it. As he stretched, the ladder tipped backward and broke. Sulley hit the ground with a crash.

The librarian spun around and charged

toward him. Sulley was dead meat!

Pop! Pop! Pop!

A loud sound made the librarian stop in her tracks. It was Don, running his suction cups on the floor to distract her! The librarian turned away from Sulley toward Don.

Then a *bang* came from the side of the room. Terri and Terry were dancing around, making an even bigger ruckus. Art began rolling around the room like a big purple wheel, laughing and yelling. The librarian was confused. She didn't know who to grab first.

At that point, the EEKs had formed a pyramid. They were just about to grab their flag when the librarian barreled past, knocking them all down.

I wanted to stay and finish the competition. But the rest of the Oozma Kappas pulled me along toward the door. The librarian charged after us, her massive tentacles waving. We barely made it outside.

"Woo-hoo!" Art yelled. "We did it!"

"No, we didn't," I told him, furious. "We forgot the flag."

"Mike," said someone behind me. I turned and saw Squishy. He held up the Oozma Kappa flag.

"How?" I asked, amazed.

Squishy just shrugged. "I guess no one noticed me."

"Misdirection," Terri added with a smile. I realized then that I might have underestimated these guys.

Oozma Kappa was still in the game.

CHAPTER 8

On our way back to the Oozma Kappa house, we ran into the PNK sorority sisters.

"Hey, are you guys going to the party?" one of them asked. They explained that there was a mixer at the ROR house. "It's for the top scare teams. You're one of us now, right?"

"Bad idea," Sulley said when they were gone.

I disagreed. "People are finally seeing us as real Scarers. We're going," I told the team.

Early that evening, we showed up at the ROR house. Unlike Squishy's mom's place, this was a real fraternity house. The place practically reeked of tradition.

As we walked through the house, the crowd at the party stared at us. Then someone shouted, "Oozma Kappa!" and everyone broke out in wild cheers. I admit, it felt pretty great.

After a while, Johnny called for everyone's attention. One by one, he congratulated all the teams that were still in the Scare Games. I stood together proudly with the Oozma Kappas.

Suddenly, the RORs ambushed us! They threw paint, glitter, and flowers at us. As a final insult, Randy pulled a rope, and cuddly toys tumbled down on our heads.

"Let's hear it for Oozma Kappa!" yelled Johnny. "The most *adorable* monsters on campus!"

The next day, a picture of the Oozma Kappas covered in glitter and stuffed animals appeared on the front page of the *Campus Roar,* the school newspaper. Even worse, the RORs had plastered copies of the humiliating photo all over campus.

When I confronted Randy, he just shrugged and said, "What do you want me to do?" He wanted to fit in with the RORs, even if it meant going along with their mean jokes.

So I marched up to Johnny. "I want you to stop making us look like fools," I told him.

"You're making yourselves look like fools," he replied with a smirk. "Let's be honest, you're never going to be real Scarers, because real Scarers look like us. But hey, if you really want to work at a scare floor, they're always hiring in the mail room." He flipped the newspaper over and pointed to a help-wanted ad. Monsters, Inc., was looking for mail-room workers.

Johnny and his ROR pals were doing everything they could to destroy our spirit—and it was working. We'd never felt worse.

"We're just embarrassing ourselves," Sulley said when the RORs were gone.

"He's right," Don agreed. "No matter how hard we train, we'll never look like them."

I felt awful. I was just beginning to believe in team Oozma Kappa, but they no longer believed in themselves. They needed inspiration. I thought I might know where to find it.

"Guys," I said. "We're going on a little field trip."

(M)

Late that night, we pulled up in front of a huge building. Ms. Squibbles, Squishy's mom, had given us a ride.

"Where are we?" Art asked.

"The big leagues," I replied. I pointed to the sign on the building: MONSTERS, INC.

Five minutes later, I'd cut through the fence and led everyone up to the roof.

We gazed down through the skylight onto the scare floor. Below us, the most talented monsters in the world were collecting screams. There were tall Scarers and short ones. Some were furry, and others had scales.

"Take a good look, fellas," I said to my team. "See what they all have in common?"

"Not really," Squishy said.

"Exactly," I said. "There's no *one* type of Scarer. The best Scarers use their differences to their advantage."

"Look!" Sulley said, pointing. "It's Screaming Bob Gunderson! I still have his rookie card."

"Me too!" I said, smiling. "You collect scare cards, huh?"

"Yep," Sulley said. "Four hundred and fifty of them."

I'd collected scare cards my whole life. It was the first time I realized that Sulley and I might actually have something in common.

Sulley sighed. "I've been a real jerk," he said.

"So have I," I admitted. "But it's not too late. We could be a great team. We just need to start working together."

From that moment on, Oozma Kappa was a real team. We trained together every morning, and we all found ways to use our talents. Soon our hard work began to pay off.

The third Scare Games challenge was called Don't Scare the Teen. We had to race through a maze while cardboard standees of children and teenagers popped out at us. The goal was to scare the kids, avoid the teenagers, and get through the maze as quickly as possible. Oozma Kappa came in second—right behind the RORs!

The next event, Hide-and-Sneak, was a hiding challenge. I'll never forget watching the referee walk right past Sulley. He was pretending to be a rug! But the true star was Don. He hid by clinging to the ceiling with his suction cups!

Against all odds—and thanks to our hard work—Oozma Kappa was still in the Scare Games. After four challenges, it was down to us and ROR.

"Enjoy the attention while it lasts," Johnny Worthington sneered. "After you lose, no one will remember you."

"Maybe," I shot back. "But when *you* lose, no one will let you forget it."

That guy was rotten to the core. I was looking forward to beating him.

CHAPTER 9

The night before the final event, I was too excited to sleep.

"We're going to win this thing tomorrow, Sulley, I can feel it!" I said.

"You know," Sulley said seriously, "you've given me a lot of really great tips. I'd love to return the favor sometime."

"Oh, sure," I said. "Anytime."

To my surprise, Sulley began to clear furniture away. He made a space in our room for us to practice.

"Okay," Sulley said, "you've memorized every textbook—and that's great. But now it's time to forget all of that. Just reach deep down and let the scary out. Go wild!"

So I did. I roared and roared.

"Bigger!" Sulley said. "Stop thinking!"

I showed him my best. "How was that?" I asked. He gave me a high five.

As I climbed into bed, I looked at my MU hat. It would be a big night tomorrow. I felt ready for it.

The next night, we showed up at the school stadium for the final Scare Games challenge. Two scare simulators had been set up. OK and ROR would compete in the simulators. The team with the highest combined scores would win.

"Be warned," the Greek Council president announced as we lined up, "each simulated scare has been set to the highest difficulty level!"

My heart pounded. The entire Monsters

University student body was there, and everyone was cheering wildly. This was the moment I'd been waiting for. It was my chance to show the whole school how scary I could be.

"First Scarers to the starting line!" the president announced.

I gathered the team. "Okay, just like we planned," I said. "I'll go first, then Don—"

"Hold on," Sulley interrupted. "Mike's the one who started all this. And I think it's only right if he's the one who finishes it."

The other OKs agreed. "Yeah, Mike!" Squishy said. "Finish strong!"

I felt a burst of pride knowing my team had so much faith in me.

I stepped aside, and Don went first. He was up against Bruiser, a huge monster from ROR. At the signal, they each charged into their own team's scare simulator. We could see what was happening inside on screens overhead.

Bruiser's scare was good. The scream can on the scoreboards filled almost halfway. But Don's scare was even better. I enjoyed the shocked look on Johnny's face when Don scored higher than Bruiser!

Watching the action, I had no doubt—the RORs were great Scarers. But we were just as good! Terri and Terry, Squishy, and Art all held their own against their ROR competitors.

Next, it was Sulley's turn. He was up against Randy. Sulley roared so loudly that both of the simulators shook and Randy flubbed his scare.

The scores were tied. Johnny and I were the only Scarers left.

It was up to me now. All my dreams were riding on this moment. I looked around and saw Hardscrabble staring at me.

"Hey," Sulley said. "You're going to prove

Hardscrabble wrong. I believe in you, buddy."

Johnny and I took our places at the starting line. The signal went off, and we ran into our simulators.

The second the door shut behind me, my training took over. I fluttered the curtains and scratched the bedframe, building my scare.

But every discouraging thing I'd ever heard kept floating through my head. Then I remembered Sulley pushing me to dig deep.

So I did. I let the scary out. I roared like I'd never roared before.

I stepped out of my scare simulator, and my

jaw dropped when I saw my score. I'd filled the can all the way to the top. I had beaten Johnny Worthington!

The place went nuts! The next thing I knew, my team was scooping me up and carrying me on their shoulders.

We had done it! Oozma Kappa had won the Monsters University Scare Games!

I was back in the Scaring Program. My life was on track again. All my dreams would finally come true.

Later, as the crowd started to break up, I went back into the scare simulator. I wanted to relive my moment of victory one last time.

Sulley followed me. "I'm gonna be a Scarer!" I told him. It still didn't seem real.

"Yes, you are," he said, grinning.

"Hear that?" I said to the robot kid. "You haven't heard the last of Mike Wazowski. Boo!"

I waggled my hands playfully.

"*Aieeeeeeeeeeeeeeeeeee!*" The robot child shot up in bed, screaming loudly. The scream can filled to the top.

"I knew I was scary," I said to Sulley, "but I didn't know I was *that* scary."

"Yeah." Sulley gave a nervous laugh. "We're so scary that I guess we broke it. Come on." He tried to get me to leave. But I knew something wasn't right.

I opened the control panel on the simulator. There were six sets of controls, one for each member of team Oozma Kappa. Each one was set to the highest difficulty—except mine. Mine was set to Easy.

No wonder I'd filled the scream can when no one else had. It wasn't because I was scarier than everyone else. It was because someone had made it easy for me. *Someone* had cheated.

"Did you do this?" I asked Sulley.

"Yes, I did, but you don't understand . . . ," Sulley began.

"Why?" I yelled. But I knew the answer. It broke my heart. "You don't think I'm scary."

From the look on Sulley's face, I could tell it was true.

"You said you believed in me," I told him.

"I just wanted to help," Sulley said.

"No, you just wanted to help yourself," I shot back.

"Well, what was I supposed to do?" Sulley

exploded. "Let the whole team fail because *you don't have it*?"

He'd finally said what he'd been thinking all along. I was sure he was wrong. But there was only one way to prove it.

I left Sulley without another word. I knew exactly what I had to do. I hurried across campus to the door lab.

The lab was shutting down for the night. When the last student left, I slipped inside. It didn't take me long to activate a door.

Security quickly realized that someone had broken in to the lab. By then I'd blocked the entrance with a cart full of scream canisters. All the guards could do was watch as I opened a door and stepped through it, into the human world.

CHAPTER 10

In the dark room, I could see a bed. There was a real, live human kid sleeping in it. Silently, I crept toward the bed. I loomed over it and roared.

The kid sat up and stared at me.

I roared again. She smiled. "You look funny," she said.

My heart sank. She didn't think I was scary. Not even a little bit.

Then I heard a cough. As I looked around, I realized that this was no bedroom. It was a cabin, and it was full of children. I had entered a sleepaway camp!

I ran out of that cabin as fast as I could. I didn't pay attention to where I was going. To be honest, I didn't care if I ever got back to Monstropolis.

I don't know how long I had been sitting at the lake near the camp when Sulley found me. I was staring at my reflection, thinking about how my whole life was a bust, when suddenly I heard Sulley's voice.

"Come on, buddy," he whispered when he saw me. "Let's get you out of here."

I didn't move. "You were right," I said. "They weren't scared of me. I did everything right. I wanted it more than anyone. And I thought if I wanted it enough, I could show everybody that Mike Wazowski is something special. But I'm just . . . not."

"I know how you feel," Sulley said.

"You do *not* know how I feel," I said angrily. "Monsters like you have everything. You'll never know what it's like to be a failure, because you were born a Sullivan!"

Sulley sighed. "Yeah," he said, "but you're not the only failure here. I act scary, Mike, but the truth is most of the time I'm terrified."

I had never seen this side of Sulley. "How come you never told me this before?" I asked.

"Because we weren't friends before," he replied.

Our conversation was interrupted by voices. The camp rangers! Sulley took off into the woods, and I found a place to hide. I watched as the rangers chased him.

He needed my help!

I caught up with Sulley as he was struggling to climb a steep slope. I helped him up and then we hurried toward the cabin. There was only one way back to Monsters University—through the closet.

The kids had been taken out of the cabin, and the rangers were still searching the forest. Sulley and I snuck into the cabin.

But when we opened the closet door, all we saw was the inside of the closet. The door back to Monsters University was gone! It had been deactivated from the monster side.

Outside, the rangers had returned to the camp. We could see their flashlight beams.

"We've got to get out of here," Sulley said.

"No," I said, thinking fast. "Let them come. If we scare them—I mean, *really* scare them—we can generate enough screams to power the door from this side. Just follow my lead."

We hid as the rangers entered the dark room. Then we began to build our scare. Sulley growled. I scurried through the shadows. Of course, the rangers didn't know who—or what—we were.

They swung their flashlights around the room, but we darted out of the way. Then we toppled a row of bunk beds, blocking the cabin door. The rangers shouted in panic. And the closet door started to glow with energy.

It was time. "Are you ready?" I asked Sulley.

He shook his head. "Mike, I can't."

"Yes, you can," I told him. "Stop being a Sullivan and start being you."

Sulley rose from the shadows and roared. He let the scary out. Boy, did he ever.

The rangers all screamed at once. It was the biggest scream I'd ever heard.

The closet door began to glow brighter and brighter, showing the way back to our world. I grabbed Sulley. We threw ourselves at the door—just as it exploded.

CHAPTER 11

I shook my head. My ears were ringing.

When my vision finally cleared, the first thing I saw was Dean Hardscrabble. She stared at us with an expression I'd never seen on her face.

"How did you do that?" she asked, stunned.

Before I could answer, the Child Detection Agency burst in. The CDA agents swarmed around us and escorted us out of the room.

I caught sight of Don, Terri and Terry, Art, and Squishy among a crowd of students. The last thing I heard as we left was Terri saying, "What's going to happen to them?"

The CDA took us directly to the Monsters

University president's office. The president wasted no time kicking us out of school. I wasn't surprised, and neither was Sulley. We knew we deserved to be kicked out for breaking the rules.

When we returned to the OK house, we delivered the bad news.

"Expelled?" Don exclaimed. He looked like he'd been slapped in the face.

"Harsh, man," Art said.

"I'm sorry, guys," I said. "You'd be in the Scaring Program right now if it weren't for us."

"Well," Don said slowly, "it's the gosh-darndest thing . . ."

"Hardscrabble's letting us into the Scaring Program!" Terry burst out. "She was impressed with our performance in the Games."

At that moment, I couldn't have been prouder than if I'd made it into the Scaring Program myself. "You're the scariest bunch of monsters

I ever met," I said. "Don't let anyone tell you different." I was going to miss them.

After we'd said our good-byes to the other OKs, Sulley and I walked together through the MU gates.

"So, what now?" Sulley asked.

"You know," I said, "for the first time in my life, I don't really have a plan."

"You're the great Mike Wazowski! You'll come up with something," said Sulley.

I smiled. "I think it's time I leave the greatness to other monsters. I'm okay with just being okay," I told him.

A bus pulled up. Sulley and I shook hands, and I climbed on board.

As the bus took off, I watched MU roll away. I saw the School of Scaring disappear in the distance . . . and with it, all my dreams.

Then, suddenly, Sulley's face appeared in my

window. He was clinging to the side of the moving bus!

"Stop the bus!" I cried. The bus lurched to a halt. I ran off and found Sulley in the street.

"Mike," Sulley said, "I don't know a single Scarer who can do what you do. You pulled off the biggest scare this school has ever seen!"

"That was you, Sulley," I pointed out.

"No," Sulley said. "That was *you*. You think I could have done that without you? Mike, you're not scary, not even a little. But you *are* fearless. And if Hardscrabble can't see that, then she can just—"

"I can just *what*?" came a voice behind us.

I nearly leaped out of my skin. When I turned around, Dean Hardscrabble was standing there. She handed me a school newspaper. "It seems you made the front page again," she said. "The two of you did something together that no one has ever

done before. You surprised me. Perhaps I should keep an eye out for more 'surprises' like you in my program."

It was a bittersweet moment. I was finally getting the respect I'd wanted all along. What a shame it was coming so late.

"But as far as you two are concerned," she went on, "there is nothing I can do for you now except wish you luck. Mr. Wazowski, keep surprising people." Then she flew off.

I looked down at the newspaper in my hand. An ad on the back caught my eye. "Help Wanted," it said. Suddenly, I had an idea.

I turned to Sulley. "There is still one way we could work on a scare floor."

We looked at each other and smiled. Right then, I knew that we would make a great team.

EPILOGUE

Our first job at Monsters, Inc., was in the mail room.

But it wasn't our last. After the mail room, we became janitors. Then they promoted us to the cafeteria. Next, we worked as scare-can wranglers. We worked hard, and our teamwork paid off, just like it had in the Scare Games.

Then the big day came—we tried out to become a scare team. With my know-how and Sulley's raw talent, we got the job.

Sulley and I were finally a real scare team.

Our first day on the job, I stood at the edge of the scare floor. I took a deep breath. This was the

moment I'd been waiting for my entire life. I could hardly believe it was real.

I looked down at my feet. There was that safety line, painted on the floor. It was the line I'd stepped over all those years ago, when I had visited Monsters, Inc., as a little monster.

Sulley walked past me onto the scare floor. "You coming, Coach?" he asked.

I stepped over the line. "You'd better believe it," I said.